Contributing Artists

Karen Brough (she, her, hers)
Author, Illustrator
Story and Oil Paintings for Cover and Chapter Openings

Iain Brough (he, him, his)
Illustrator
Pen & Ink Drawings of Bears and Border Design for "Ostara" Oil Painting

Leslie Brough (they, them, their)
Illustrator
Pen & Ink Drawings of Celtic Border Knots and Heart-Knot Basket

Aurora Books, an imprint of Eco-Justice Press, L.L.C.

Aurora Books
P.O. Box 5409 Eugene, OR 97405
www.ecojusticepress.com

Young Bear
Story by Karen Brough with Illustrations by Karen Brough, Iain Brough & Leslie Brough

Library of Congress Control Number: 2016960867
ISBN 978-1-945432-55-2

First printing March, 2023
Revised December, 2023

This Beltale, inspired by the gentle timbre of my mother's voice, is our gift to Green Man, my husband, John W. Brough, Jr., with gratitude, respect and love everlasting, and in memory of our beloved friend, Patrick Frye, 1940-2021, who, in my father's absence, provided grandfatherly love to our children. Patrick, the ever intrepid eco-justice warrior, proud of both his Celtic and Native American ancestry, is missed by all who knew and loved him.

Beltane

Enchanted moonlight, mystic bliss

Engender true love's genesis

In April, vernal showers rain

Come fruit tree blossom with Beltane

Intention at the wishing well

Commence a courtship ritual

'Tis early morning in the midst of spring, the time when love fills the air and promise is alive in the warm glow of Earth's transformation. Migratory birds have returned to grace us with song. Woodland creatures tend their homes and their young while butterflies and other insects mingle with faeries in dappling beams of light. Beaver appears to explore the neighborhood and examine his lodge. Mother Raccoon rinses succulent greens in a stream as her litter awaits breakfast. Dragonfly and Sylph skim the water and join the faerie ring.

It is May first on the wheel of the year, the holy day pagans name Beltane. Today the veil between the earthly and spirit worlds is thin. This is a time of magic and romance. The days outlast the nights by some, as several weeks have passed since equinox. Pagans gather to celebrate the strong connection between the realms. They take offerings and intentions to bubbling springs, watering holes, and wishing wells. Dressed in airy, loose garments, they dance around the Maypole and beseech Mother Earth for blessings of new life.

Young Bear is a maiden black bear. She has wandered some distance from the safety of her mother's reach. At two years, she has grown strong and independent, though her humble heart endears her to the woodlands. Her new love, Wind Runner, is well matched with her. He too lives quietly among creatures of the woods. They are playful with each other. He is gentle in their courtship. Together they spend their

nights on the back side of Hurricane Mountain. They hunt for leaves and grubs and delight in the sweet scent of lilac and apple blossom. Occasionally, they stir midday, bathing in a pool refreshed by waterfall.

On this day, the bears do not rest long by the water. Pagans have arrived to commence Beltane festivities. An elder checks the smoldering coals from last night's blaze. Others work together sorting red and white ribbons for the pole. Children laugh and play as they search for enchanted beings. A young couple dances atop a stoic boulder, respectfully known as Old Gran. Sun lights the copper and gold strands of the woman's hair. Her husband slowly turns her toward him. He kneels to put his ear to her belly. She is not yet showing.

For a moment, Young Bear and Wind Runner silently observe the revelers from the shadow of cedar boughs. The bears know these visitors mean no harm, but they remain hidden. Animal and plant communities reside in a state of reverence for all life, but humans are able to sever such awareness with a powerful sense of self-importance. For this reason, Young Bear and Wind Runner fear them, as do the other creatures of the woods.

Litha

Light endowed Father Sun

He doth shine o'er everyone

Celebrate a time of vision

Earth procures her labors' mission

Now his torch begins to fade

Thanks we give, farewell bade

The petals of Trillium have fallen. Spring has passed and Rooster greets his brightest morn. 'Tis summer solstice, and her name is Litha. Father Sun brings forth his longest day as Mother Earth comes into her fullest phase of motherhood. Though his light has nurtured her back to life, it is her wisdom to turn from her consort. She cannot remain in his brightest shine lest his strength should overcome her and leave her scorched and desert.

Young Bear and Wind Runner have remained companions throughout the last days of spring. It is unusual for Eastern black bears to stay together after mating, but this pair lingers. Together they roll in a sun filled daisy meadow or nuzzle affections, cleaning honey from each other's nose. Yet with the transition to Litha, Young Bear begins to slip away from Wind Runner. Just as the great matron Earth subtly withdraws from her Lord Sun, Young Bear turns away from Wind Runner to tend to her needs and those of her unborn cubs.

On this day of summer solstice, pagans thank Sun God and bid him farewell. They celebrate with bonfire and commune with drum and dance, collecting energy for productivity and growth. Farmers lend hand to each other, bringing in the first crop of hay. Young girls weave garland of Saint John's wort and Virginia creeper to ward off faerie mischief and protect the health of their livestock.

The bears' time together diminishes. They busy themselves, foraging for berries and insects. They shall not squander this time. It is their chance to prepare for winter, time to gain the protective layers necessary for survival.

At the farmhouse, pagans join in circle. The farmer's wife lights a torch. So turns the wheel of the year, transitioning from one season to the next…

Lughnasadh

Cast thine eyes upon the field

Her body tires as she doth yield

Mother gives and so depletes

Bloom recedes in barren heats

She turns from him to save herself

All life depends upon her health

Shun his light, his love betray

Lost affections go astray

August second on the wheel of the year, 'tis the holy day Lughnasadh, first of three major harvest celebrations. This is a time of joy and abundance as Earth delivers her bounty. A busy morning at the farmhouse, the kitchen is lively with food preparation. From the garden comes a woman carrying a basket filled with cucumber and dill. A gentle man holds open the screen door. Dishwater drips from his hands. Suds soak the thirsty old floor planks.

By midday, guests arrive and musical instruments are tuned. Two men assemble a stage for puppetry and dance. The older boys and girls practice poetry and song. Little ones stay in their swimsuits all day, dashing under the farmer's hose when they get the chance. There is laughter in the slow, warm wind.

It is several weeks since last the bears were together. Dawn arrives and Young Bear is weary after an active night of foraging. She is near her resting tree, but the hollow cavity beneath the old Ash does not call to her today. Instead, she settles on a soft carpet of club moss and stag horn lichen.

Wind Runner's home range spans an area with a diameter of fifteen miles. His turf encompasses Young Bear's smaller home range. Of late, he has foraged the outskirts of his range, but today he has roamed within three or four miles of Young Bear. He stops on a rocky shelf to survey this familiar ground. A warm breeze brushes against his muzzle. He catches scent of Young Bear. He has missed her. It does not take him long to find her. He snorts and rubs his shoulder against her back. Over she rolls, stretching and smiling with a whiney yawn. She has missed him as well.

A short distance from the woodlands and the farmlands, two strangers arrive in the village. They stop at the small country store to stock up on provisions. Their inconspicuous attire of denim and flannel is not likely to draw attention. Barely noticed by the locals, they pull a few cans of food from the shelves.

Their pickup truck is at least ten years old, dried mud splatter caked to the wheel wells. A thick olive-green canvass secured with rope conceals their gear. One of the men is quiet and avoids eye contact with the clerk. The other looks up and smiles. He is oddly unsettling, but he means no harm to her. These men have come for bear.

Men have hunted bear for thousands of years, sacrificing the noble beast for its gall bladder. This small internal organ produces bile, a bitter greenish-yellow fluid that is used in ancient healing remedies. Bile from any mammal yields the same medicinal properties. And the discarded gall bladder of domestic livestock is readily available, virtually indistinguishable from bear gall bladder, yet it is bear's bitter fluid that commands a high price on the black market. Perhaps it is the conquest of a great creature that man seeks, a creature of powerful spirit that he hopes to possess.

Three picnic tables end to end make ample seating to accommodate all. Two women spread tablecloths. Three boys follow with serving bowls and platters. One boy and two girls carry stacks of plates, a basket of utensils, and a pile of napkins. A steady flow of prepared food comes from the kitchen. Everyone finds a place at the table.

At the base of the mountain, a dirt road pulls away from the main route, leading to an overgrown lane tucked away and seldom used. The strangers discovered it late last fall as foliage drifted and the cut was revealed. The quiet man drives the rambling truck. The one who smiles looks back through the rear window, gear is secure. A cloud of dust chases after them.

Young Bear and Wind Runner bathe in their favorite swimming pool before curling around each other on the warm and expansive surface of Old Gran. Sun dries their fur as they surrender to fatigue. Soon Young Bear stirs and lifts her head. The strangers are near. The man who smiles baits a trap with animal fat as the quiet one keeps watch.

At the tables, guests are seated. Children giggle and pinch each other. Men talk and laugh. The farmer's wife stands to settle the crowd, "Thank you all for being here today at our first harvest celebration. We offer grace to Mother Earth and Father Sun…"

Young Bear slides from the rock and attempts to run. Her lumbering body does not make quick escape. Wind Runner lifts his heavy head and groans. He beckons Young Bear. She turns to face him before closing her eyes.

A few drops of rain begin to sprinkle on the feast. The farmer turns his head toward the mountain. His wife continues, "We offer gratitude for the blessings before us…"

The strangers have heard Wind Runner. They are closer than they had thought. They listen and move swiftly in the direction of the groan. Raindrops hurry.

The guests rise from their seats, taking each other's hands. They look up into the rain. The matron speaks once more, "Blessed all, blessed be."

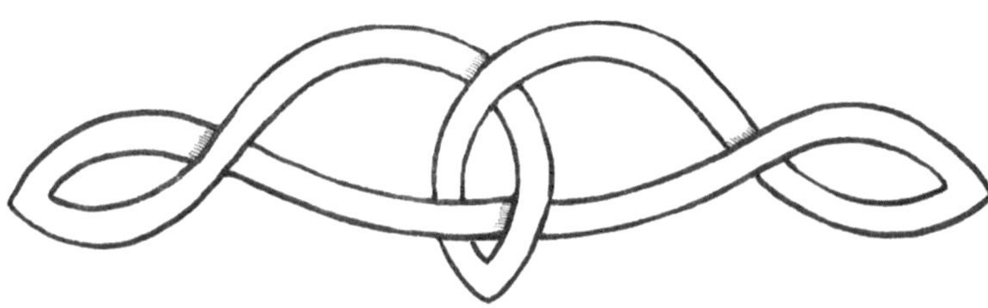

Wind Runner stands as he howls after Young Bear. The sky withdraws and down pours rain. He relents and circles back on the surface of the rock. A thunderous clap booms.

A clear shot takes Wind Runner.
The strangers are still.
The quiet one lowers his gun.

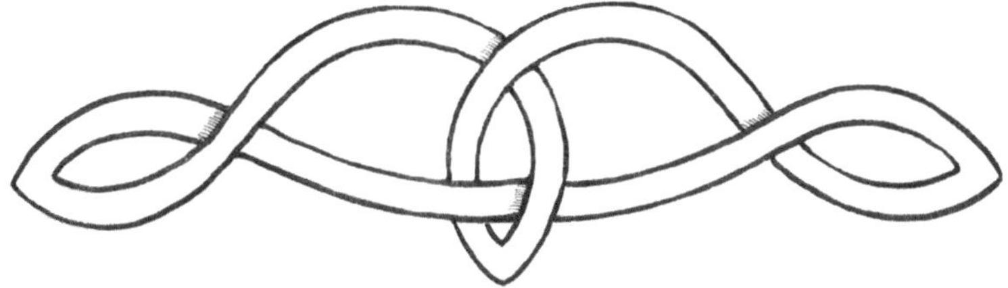

Mabon

Even days, colors blaze

In harmony and peace we gaze

We pay homage to the King

For blessed harvest he doth bring

Earth sets forth the season's feast

Morning gold rise in the east

Bestow their gifts with our gratitude

Sun shall set in solitude

Leaves turn and symmetry provides order in measured rhythm. It is autumnal equinox, a time of balance as the hours of light equal the night. The community celebrates Mabon, the second major harvest and gathering of grace. It has been a good growing season. The farmer is grateful and rests assured as Sun God continues his descent. Ivy, a symbol of healing, crawls high on the Poplar. Time to repair the shingles on the barn. Young Bear's heart begins to mend.

Samhain

Collect a ring of hazelnut

And so create an amulet

'Tis her time to be alone

Become the aspect of a crone

Bear winds down around her breath

Her body slows, she mimics death

Ancestors call from another world

Invite encounter, path is furled

Introspection, journey home

Descend to dark, transcend this realm

Wind blows through bare limbs of hallowed woods. An eerie rattle stirs echoes of retreat. Death fills the void with the presence of all souls. It is late October on the wheel of the year. Halcyon days have passed. Tonight is Samhain, final harvest is complete. Again, the veil between earthly and spirit worlds is thin. Spirits of deceased loved ones are near. Pagans celebrate the last major harvest with a feast for the dead at the old farmhouse. Pumpkins carved into lanterns light the way. Bread and wine are offered to the otherworldly guests.

Cool evenings and diminishing daylight lay siege to communities of the wild. Hearty evergreens continue to photosynthesize throughout winter while torpid vegetation seeks refuge within the womb. It is said that any crops not harvested by Samhain should be left in the fields to appease the gods and baneful faeries. As food supplies dwindle, some bird species flee. Abiding creatures heed the winged harbingers and follow complex plans to survive the cold.

Young Bear makes way for her inner sanctum. She has prepared her den beneath the old Ash. There she will hibernate for months without eating, drinking, or passing waste. Her heavy pelt and fatty layer should provide ample insulation and sustenance for her own survival, pray too for the nourishment of her unborn cubs. Unsure how her littles have fared, she has lined the den with additional debris.

A cool damp night convinces the farmer to light a fire in the wood stove. Guests will appreciate the warmth as they arrive. The farmer's wife lifts their toddling granddaughter who perches instinctively on her Nanna's hip. Together grandmother and child peer through the kitchen window. The midwife has arrived at the small cottage next door.

Young Bear finds comfort within the confines of her winter nook. Her body and mind quiet. She slips into unconsciousness, lulled to sleep by the languid rhythm of her heart, deeper and deeper she settles into the realm of spirit world.

The midwife, at Sylwin's beside, gently applies a stethoscope to the expectant mother's belly. "This baby is strong." Sylwin sweeps a lock of her copper and gold hair behind her ear. She smiles as she reaches for her husband's hand, "Do you want to listen, Gael?" He has been attentive throughout the midwife's careful examination. He smiles as he takes Sylwin's hand.

Within her hibernation dream-state, Young Bear journeys the spirit world, roaming through ethereal passageways before entering the enchanted realm. An entwined and knotted network of luminous roots creates dimly lit, winding corridors. Young Bear spies a gnarled branch among the roots above her. It slips free and lands on the earthen floor ahead. Upon impact, the twisted limb transforms into Snake, who weaves her way forward. She is Young Bear's guide on this otherworldly journey.

Young Bear follows Snake without question or expectation. Soon they enter a mystical forest. Three playful cubs tumble down a gently sloping bank into view. Snake slithers around the base of a tree encouraging Young Bear to settle and observe. Young Bear is reminded that she remains unknowing of whether she has prepared well enough to nourish her unborn cubs to term.

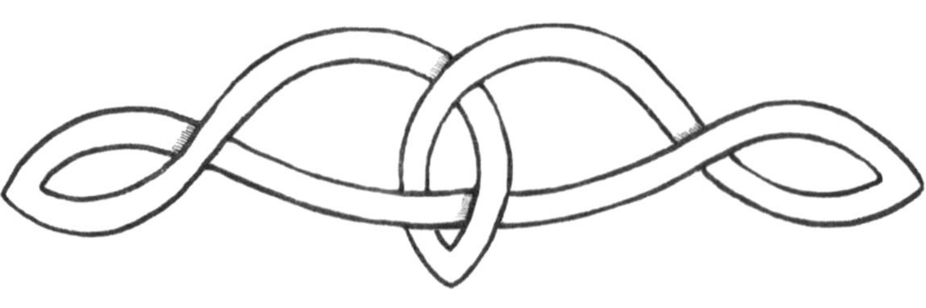

A mother bear must gain full winter weight before hibernation to ensure the survival of her cubs. Young Bear foraged diligently throughout the spring and early summer. But she was mournful and lethargic after Wind Runner's death. She is aware that if she has failed to build sufficient fat reserves, her unborn cubs may not survive.

Upon completion of the prenatal visit, midwife and expectant couple join the Samhain festivities at the farmhouse. A large group of family and friends gather in circle under a full moon. The farmer's wife calls upon the Cardinal directions...North, South, East, and West, inviting all spirits and otherworldly guests.

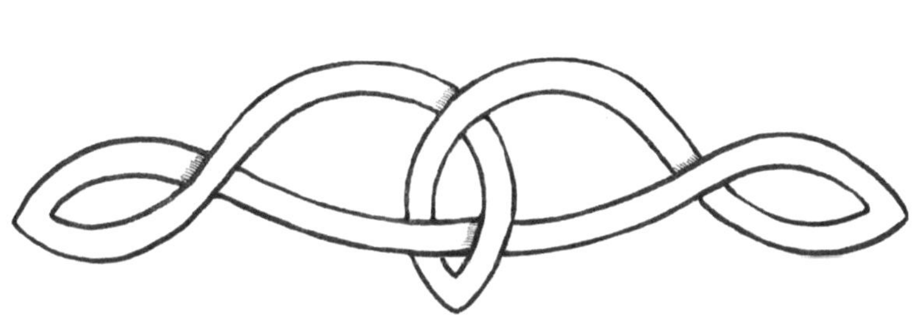

Yule

Cometh snow, white fall to Earth

A gentle blanket protects rebirth

Wind with pirouette and bow

Encircles her, and snow doth plow

Here is Yule, deep night of year

Dull drum heartbeat in her ear

Rake the embers of the fire

Celebrate as dreams transpire

For this day marks shift in light

Henceforth, encroach upon the night

Winter solstice, known as Yule, marks the longest night of the year. On this day, morning light comes later and evening falls earlier than on any other day. At dusk, the diminishing old Sun God retires to his death. In passing, he makes way for the birth of the new infant God of Light who shall rise the next morning and grow in strength and brilliance with each day to come. Revelers say final farewells to the old and rejoice in the birth of the new Sun King.

Hibernation continues Young Bear's spirit journey. She basks in warm light on the surface of Old Gran, hearing soft music reverberating in the cascade of waterfall. Snake slips over Young Bear's shoulder, winding 'round her body. Her eyes open slowly, and he is there. Wind Runner sits before Young Bear, holding her in his gaze. She shakes her head with a disbelieving wide grin, then leans forward to nudge him with the back of her neck. He is there. She can see him, but touch is different in spirit world. Hollowness often endures. For a moment, Young Bear is filled with grief and disappointment until Wind Runner's love overcomes the barrier between time and space, life and death, spirit and flesh, overwhelming her with gentle embrace. Then, once again, she is grateful.

Evergreen trees signify eternal life. The farmer carries a freshly cut balsam fir into the main living area of the farmhouse. His wife untangles a string of lights as their granddaughter opens a box of Yule decorations. The house is made festive with elvish finery, holly, and mistletoe. The small lights on the tree represent the return of Sun and the rekindling of his relationship with Earth.

Guests arrive at the farmhouse with merriment and cheer, exchanging candles as a symbol of new light. The farmer's eyes twinkle as he smiles at his wife. The community is filled with anticipation, excitement, and hope. The midwife, already next door, has come to assist with the birth. Magic abounds. Gods willing, a new baby shall arrive on this sacred night.

Gael guides Sylwin with deep and expansive breath. Each contraction, like a wave, builds, intensifies, and then subsides. Sylwin eases herself into the calmness she has practiced. She begins to give herself over to her own laboring body, each breath allowing her to find courage and release doubt. She ambles through the cottage, midwife and Gael on either side. The midwife reassures, "You are safe, Sylwin... the baby is safe...trust your body and the love around you."

Young Bear and Wind Runner sit nose to nose on Old Gran. Each taking in the other, inhaling and exhaling as a comforting current flows between them.

Sylwin stands with feet wide, grasping the post at the foot of her bed. The contraction is strong, knees buckling, hand slipping the length of the post until she is on the floor on her hands and knees. She directs expansive breath into her body, releasing tension from her core to birth canal. Gael speaks in a tender tone, "The baby's head is out." His words touch Sylwin like a welcome cue, and she bears down into the pressure of a final uterine contraction. Effortless, the baby slips from her body.

Gael cradles the newborn in his arms. The midwife helps Sylwin to the bed. Carefully, the new father places the little one to Sylwin's chest. New mother rests her hand gently on the infant's back. There is joy. There are tears. 'Tis Yule and a son is born.

Imbolc

Mother we hold dear to you, and still we have grown thin

Isolation near exhausts resources from within

Meager is our sustenance, survival tenuous

Relentless are the darkest days, Sun exiguous

They called to us to say He'd come, deliver us erelong

Now, dear midwife, it is time, heart is growing strong

Could it be the King arrives in time we may revive?

Doth His flame ignite in us desire to survive?

Some pass not another moon, yet ours shall not forlorn

Hope inspires life anew, an infant to adorn

Despite the promise of Sun, the weeks following winter solstice are increasingly difficult, accruing daylight barely discernible for too long. At Yule, fat reserves and wood supplies were plentiful, but as the calendar turns toward midwinter, provisional shortages are felt. Insistent birds and insects shiver mercilessly. Small animals such as Woodchuck and Ground Squirrel awaken every few days to fill their bellies. Those without ample food stores will perish.

Imbolc, the holy day falling on February second on the wheel of the year, is considered the crossroads of winter. Finally, the increase in daylight becomes apparent. At this time, the mounting frustrations of the season reach a precipice before tiny rays of hope begin to glimmer on the horizon. Now comes Imbolc, quickening the coming of light. With a welcome sense of relief and delight, pagans notice Sun rising earlier and setting later each day. At long last, winter begins to yield.

The cottage is warm with logs ablaze in the fireplace. Sylwin and Gael are cozy in their home with Baby in the cradle.

Sun burns orange in a pink and purple sky. A large great horned owl streaks across the horizon, weaving her way down toward a cove. She perches on a stony ridge along the water's edge. As she lands, the honorable bird transforms into a high priestess. She has the face of an owl though her body is human form, clothed in feathered gown. The priestess bows her head and wraps her wings, like a cloak, around her graceful figure. She is here to escort spirits of woodland creatures back to the light in communal crossing ceremony. She lifts her head enough to gaze upon the water's surface. Her wings unfurl loosely, billowing low. Iridescent mist swirls like wisps of smoke on the water, scrying illusion...an old fox, small birds, grandmother doe...all drifting, dancing upward toward the orange ball of fire.

Those who have not survived the harsh season pass through the light into the spirit world, the creative realm, the world accessed through dream, contemplation, and imaginings. None have died in vain. In passing, all immerse within the domain of ever expanding, holy consciousness. Each transcends with individual spirit intact, coinciding as part of the whole…preserved enlightenment of the sentient universe. All knowledge, discoveries, and solutions recorded. All growth, development, and change experienced during life archived in collective memory and guiding conscience for the purpose of eternal inspiration...the driving force of creation, innovation, and evolution.

As the ceremonial crossing wave subsides, the priestess graciously bows her head in silence before extending her wings and taking flight.

Within the confines of her inner sanctum, Young Bear's eyes give flicker. Her breath quickens as her body prepares to give birth. Expectant female black bears awaken briefly at Imbolc into an omniscious state, the transboundary space connecting the earthly and spirit realms within the borderlands of duality. Young Bear is simultaneously aware of her stiff and sluggish body in the dark, cramped space of the den as well as the comforting presence of spirit, the great midwife, Mother Earth. Her heartbeat grows in strength. Protective layers have sustained her and proven ample to nourish the cubs to term. Now, at the crossroads of winter, birthing time is here.

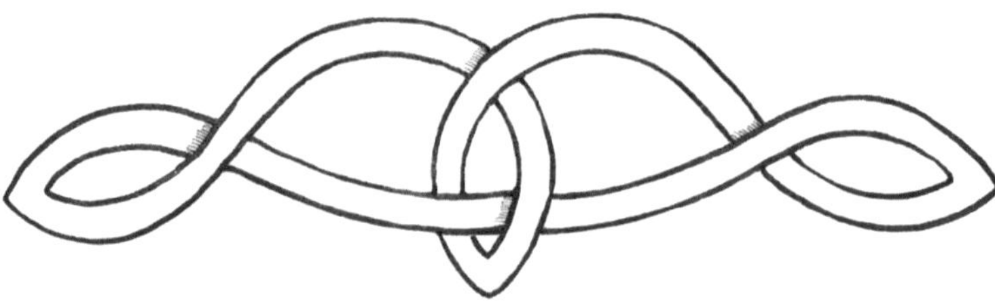

The farmer's wife lights a candle and sets it on the window sill to coax Sun's return. Hope and gratitude spread throughout the community.

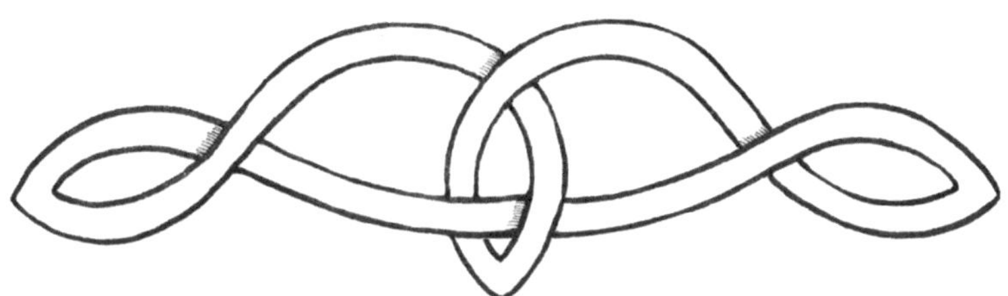

In her den, Young Bear stirs without fear, giving herself over to a power greater than her own. She is gracious, she is holy. No longer a maiden, she is now Mother Bear.

Ostara

Alas she aches to feel his touch

He warms her now with light as such

In gratitude, her tears do flow

And rivers flood with melting snow

Life revealed, sheep is shorn

Behold her beauty, Earth reborn

After birthing the cubs, Mother Bear drifts back into hibernation. She must endure the last weeks of winter with the least amount of effort. The cubs, weighing less than a pound each at birth, do not hibernate. They remain close to their mother, gaining nourishment and warmth from her body.

The twentieth of March marks the first day of spring at the vernal equinox. Pagans celebrate the holy day of Ostara. Like the autumnal equinox, it is a day of balance, harmony restored with equal hours of daylight and darkness. Warm weather arrives early this year, Clintonia and Trout Lily already in bloom. Sylwin and Gael hike to the mountain pool for an early morning celebration with Baby.

Nearing the end of her hibernation journey, Mother Bear sees herself and Wind Runner in a field of Lupine. The playful cubs chase butterflies and faeries. Mother Bear is at peace knowing winter's end has come. Spring is here, time to return to the earthly realm. Her heart drums softly, calling her home. The cubs nuzzle and nip their father. She is warmed by the tenderness between them.

Mother Bear longs to be with her cubs, to feel their touch in the physical world. The drum gains strength and resonance. Snake reappears to guide her back through the ethereal corridors. There is no delay, no plodding through return journey. Drum beats hard, fast, and furious, and Mother Bear runs as swiftly as the wind.

Waking in her den, Mother Bear stretches and draws in a deep breath. She smells Earth, the cubs, and life.

Sylwin rests on a handwoven blanket strewn over the sunny surface of Old Gran. Gael sits beside her with Baby in his arms. The child is healthy with dark curls like his father.

Mother Bear nudges her cubs. They have grown restless, anxious to leave the confines of the den. The burliest of the three boldly tumbles from the winter nook. Two smaller cubs follow. For the first time, they see the light of day, smell the scent of fresh air, feel the warmth of Sun on their growing bodies. Moments later, with yawning groan and blinking eyes, Mother Bear emerges from the quiet refuge beneath the old Ash.

From high upon Old Gran, Baby's attention is drawn to the woods. "What does he see?" Sylwin asks. "I don't know, maybe he hears something," Gael replies. Baby laughs and claps his hands, aware of forest creatures and spirits of the woods. He crinkles his nose and grins with twinkling eyes.

Author's Reading List
Recommended for Nature Holidays
Background & Rituals...

A Year of Ritual
Sabbats & Esbats for
Solitaries & Covens
Sandra Kynes
Copyright ©2004
Llewellyn Publications

Paganism
An Introduction to
Earth-Centered Religions
Joyce & River Higginbotham
Copyright ©2002
Llewellyn Publications

Advanced Celtic Shamanism
D.J. Conway
Copyright ©2000
The Crossing Press

Sabbats
A Witch's Approach to
Living the Old Ways
Edain McCoy
Copyright ©1994
Llewellyn Publications

Animal Speak
The Spiritual & Magical Powers
of Creatures Great & Small
Ted Andrews
Copyright ©1993
Llewellyn Publications

Medicine Cards
Jamie Sams & David Carson
Copyright ©1988
St. Martin's Press

The Way of the Shaman
Michael Harner
Copyright ©1980, 1990
HarperSanFrancisco
A Division of
HarperCollinsPublishers